Kiki's Journey

Enjoy
the
journey!

Story by
Kristy Orona-Ramirez

Illustrations by
Jonathan Warm Day

Children's Book Press   San Francisco, California

California Tribes

Yurok
Maidu
Pomo
Chumash

"Today I'd like to talk about California Indians," said Mrs. Lee. "Kristina, is there anything that you can tell us about Native Californians?"

I felt a red heat spread across my face. "No, not really. Sorry," I said and lowered my head. Just because my parents were born on a reservation, she expects me to know everything about all Native Americans.

Hilda Garcia leaned over and whispered, "What about all the stuff you have at home? Why didn't you tell Mrs. Lee about that?"

"It's not California Indian stuff. It's Tiwa, from Taos Pueblo," I said. If Mrs. Lee had asked me about my parent's tribe, I could have brought my pueblo drum or my woven sash to class. But she didn't.

"I hate it!" I roared to my mother after school. "I hate that everyone thinks I know everything about all Indians!"

I looked around my room. My cradleboard and all of my moccasins from the time I was a baby hung above my bed.

"Kiki, people ask questions because they really don't know. They are just trying to understand a way of living that is very different from their own. That doesn't make it right or wrong. It just means that they don't understand," Mom said as she stroked my hair. "Let's think about how you can tell people how you feel in a good way."

My mother led me out to the backyard by the hand. As the sun warmed our faces she said softly, "Creator, we offer this prayer to you so that we can be reminded of the Red Road that we must follow here in this city. We offer our prayers to the four directions. Help us and guide us on this journey through life. Help us to be kind and generous when we have nothing. Help us to forgive when we have been wronged, and, Creator, please help us to grow into the kind of people that you would hope for us to be."

I closed my eyes and let the words come into my heart as the wind danced around us.

A week later, for my spring break, my family left for Taos. I had only been to the Pueblo once, when I was a baby, and I couldn't remember a thing about the place.

Our drive lasted two days, through the Arizona desert and into New Mexico. My dad played old tapes of Pow Wow music. He turned to my mother and sang along:

"You are my love, way ya heah haya,
Beautiful as a mountain flower
The beautiful mountain flower
Waya ha waya hayaaa..."

My mother blushed as I smiled and hummed along. Eventually I
could see the outline of the Pueblo against the horizon, as the dust
of the desert curled in clouds behind our truck.

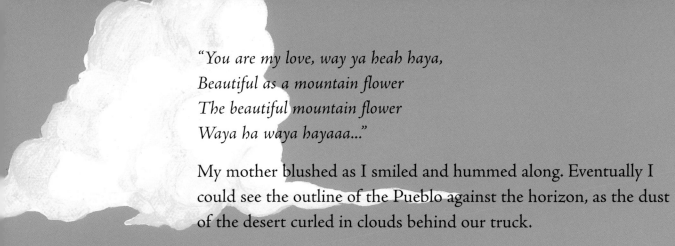

We parked by an old adobe church. We sat in the car for a minute and let a song of silence pass between us. I thought about Grandma Santana and Uncle Tim, and how it had been such a long time since I had seen them. I closed my eyes and thought to myself, "Creator, let this be a good trip for all of us."

My thoughts were interrupted by a knock on the car window. "*Hee-yah-hoo!* Hello! Come out and give Grandma a hug and a kiss!" I opened my eyes and saw my grandmother's soft wrinkled face curled up in a friendly smile through the window of the truck. I opened the door and was instantly scooped up by Grandma and Uncle Tim, who both smothered me in thousands of kisses.

11

Early the next morning I woke up to the sounds of wood crackling and pots and pans bumping into each other. Rubbing the sleep out of my eyes, I walked into the kitchen.

"Good morning, sleepyhead! Time to bake some oven bread outside. Wash your hands and put this on." Grandma Santana handed me an apron and waddled over to a bowl of red chilies soaking in water. She didn't have a toaster or a microwave. She made everything from scratch and by hand.

Mom was working some dough on a floured tablemat. "Come on Kiki, we haven't got all day! We need this bread made by lunch time."

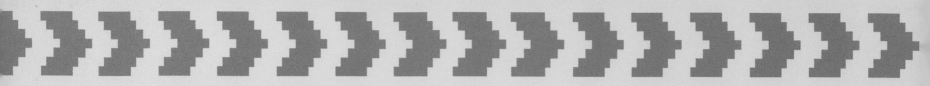

"Are we are going to bake it in that?" I pointed to the adobe oven outside the house.

"Yep. I haven't baked bread in years—come on, you've got to learn how to do it," Mom said, smiling. "Can't be Tiwa and not know how to bake bread! And I was thinking, maybe tomorrow you can go take a tour of the Pueblo."

"Take a tour? Like the tourists?" I asked as I slowly put on the apron that my Grandma had given me. "Can't you or Uncle Tim take me around?"

Mom shook her head. "Uncle Tim is working and I'll be busy with your Grandma. Don't look so worried! It's a beautiful time of year to see the village. You'll be okay."

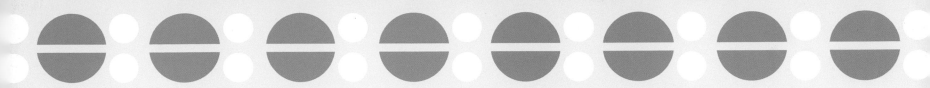

The next afternoon, I walked slowly to the center of the Pueblo. Butterflies of every color swirled around in my stomach as I read a sign that hung in front of a small adobe building:

PUEBLO TOURS
No cameras or photography
No recording or videotaping
No sketching or painting

I joined a small group of people who had gathered to take the tour. I smiled nervously at a blond boy who looked about my age. He wrinkled up his nose at me and whispered to another kid beside him. They both stared at me, but neither one smiled back.

As we walked through the village, I learned about the Blue Lake, which had been taken from the Tiwa by the U.S. government in 1906. The People fought hard to have the Blue Lake returned to them, and in 1970, it was. For generations of Tiwa, the Lake has remained a special place for sacred ceremonies.

We walked inside the San Geronimo chapel where an old woman sat quietly in a pew with her rosary beads. Afterwards, outside, I listened to our guide talk about life on the Pueblo. I remembered my mother's stories of growing up here.

Old memories of my mother's stories and the new sights around me mixed in my heart.

After the tour, Grandma Santana met me outside the gift shop. I held her soft, wrinkled hand in mine as we walked through the village.

"Well, what did you think? We have a beautiful village here, don't we?" she asked.

"You sure do, Grandma. You're lucky," I said. Grandma stopped and looked at me.

"What do you mean, *I* am lucky?" she said. "This village belongs to you, too. *We* are lucky, Kiki. So many of our ancestors have worked so hard to keep this place for our people. And not just for me or for you, but for the generations of Tiwa to come."

I looked into her eyes, feeling a little embarrassed. "But it's been so long since I've been here, Grandma. I don't even remember it." I wondered how Grandma felt about Mom, Dad, and me living so far away, trying to be Tiwa and living in the city at the same time.

We stopped by the little creek that flowed through the Pueblo. Grandma pulled me close.

"I remember when your mom and dad told me that they had to leave the Pueblo. I didn't know why the Creator would let my daughter and her husband leave. So I prayed. And then one day I realized something."

I wasn't sure why, but tears filled my eyes.

"The Creator has a job for each one of us, Kiki. For some of us, He chooses the life of a potter, of learning to shape clay for the People. Some of us become medicine people who learn how to help heal the sick. He may bless us with the gift of weaving or farming. And for some of us, He chooses a life of learning from books and studying in universities. This is the kind of life the Creator has chosen for your mother and father, and maybe for you, too, Kiki."

I hugged Grandma close and let the tears spill out. As I hugged her, she sang a song in Tiwa. I felt the love we had for each other pass between us with every warm heartbeat we shared.

"I love you, Grandma."

"I love you too, Kiki. I am so proud of you." She kissed my cheek. "Remember that even though you are far away, living in that big city, always be proud of this place and who you are. That is the best gift that you can give to yourself and to the Creator, the best gift for all of us."

Then Grandma smiled and said, "Now, how about we go home and see if today's bread is about done?"

Back at the house, Mom had set the table and wrapped the fresh bread in a clean dishtowel to keep it warm. The house was filled with the smells of good cooking.

As I helped bring dinner to the table, I looked around the room at Mom's old *manta*, turquoise jewelry, and pictures of Mom and Uncle Tim when they were little. They both stood frozen in time, their faces shiny after dancing all day at a Corn Dance years ago. My baby picture hung close by. I could see in the old photos how much I looked like Mom when she was a kid.

The night before we were to leave the Pueblo to go back home to Los Angeles, Uncle Tim and Grandma sat and ate red chili stew with us. We laughed as Mom, Dad, and Uncle Tim told me about when they were my age. They laughed about the time Uncle Tim got chased by one of the reservation dogs.

As everyone laughed and remembered, I excused myself from the dinner table and slipped out the front door. I wanted to see the village one more time before we left to go back to the city.

As I walked through the village, I felt a cool breeze two-step through my hair. I thought about my parents' hearts belonging to both the Pueblo and the city, and I knew then that mine did too.

As the starry blanket of night spread itself across the sky, I whispered, "Thank you, Creator. Thank you for this beautiful day and this safe journey home."

30

A note from the author

Kiki's Journey is a lot like my own first visit to Taos. Kiki is an urban Indian, like me, who takes a journey back home to her reservation for the first time and comes away from it with the knowledge that her people will never forget her. As in many Native cultures, she is part of the collective memory of the people and the land.

It is my hope that we all cherish the experiences of other people, that we are humbled by the different roads we decide to travel, the places we encounter, and the people we meet along the way. Enjoy the journey.

All my relations,
Kristy Orona-Ramirez
Taos Pueblo/Tarahumara

Glossary

Adobe – A sun-dried mixture of clay and straw.

Cradleboard – A transportable baby carrier, usually made of wood or basketry with cloth or leather ties. Each Native tribe has their own traditional way to carry their infants.

Manta – Part of a Pueblo woman's traditional dance attire.

Oven bread – Bread that is baked in a traditional dome-shaped adobe oven; sometimes also called *horno* bread.

Pueblo drum – A drum made from a hollowed-out aspen or cottonwood log and rawhide, used to announce ceremonies and joyous gatherings. Drum making and the tanning of deer hides is a specialty of Taos Pueblo.

Red Road – A Native American cultural attitude that involves leading a positive and responsible lifestyle.

Reservation – After taking Native peoples' tribal lands, the US Government set aside certain parcels of land for individual tribes, called reservations. On a reservation, tribal government has the authority to govern its own people, and communicates with the United States Government like another nation would. Not all Native people live on reservations.

The patterns you see on the pages of this book are of Pueblo and Plains tribal origin, from a collection of abstracted patterns that are available for public domain usage. Thanks to Wiz Allred of Desert Moon Graphics for providing them.

Story © 2006 by Kristy Orona-Ramirez
Illustrations © 2006 by Jonathan Warm Day

Editor: Dana Goldberg
Design & Production: Carl Angel

Special thanks to Ana Elba Pavón of the San Mateo Public Library, Rosalyn Sheff, Giovanna Paponetti, and the staff of Children's Book Press.

Library of Congress Cataloging-in-Publication Data

Orona-Ramirez, Kristy,
Kiki's journey / story by Kristy Orona-Ramirez; illustrations by Jonathan Warm Day.
    p. cm.
Summary: When eight-year-old Kiki travels to Taos Pueblo, the reservation where her parents grew up, she confronts her identity as both a Tiwa Indian and a big city girl.
Includes bibliographical references and index.

ISBN-13: 978-0-89239-214-8 (alk. paper)
ISBN-10: 0-89239-214-2 (alk. paper)

[1. Tiwa Indians—Fiction. 2. Indians of North America—New Mexico—Fiction. 3. Identity—Fiction.] I. Warm Day, Jonathan, ill. II. Title.

PZ7.O648Kik 2006

[E]—dc22   2005032960

Distributed to the book trade by Publishers Group West. Quantity discounts available through the publisher for educational and nonprofit use.

Printed in Singapore by Tien Wah Press
10 9 8 7 6 5 4 3 2

Children's Book Press is a nonprofit publisher of multicultural and bilingual children's picture books. For a free catalog, write to us at Children's Book Press, 2211 Mission Street, San Francisco, CA 94110. Visit us on the web at:
    www.childrensbookpress.org

Kristy Orona-Ramirez

(Taos Pueblo/Tarahumara) has been writing short stories and poetry since she was seven years old. A writer and fourth grade teacher, Kristy is also a lead singer and song-writer for the Native American Northern drumming group, The Mankillers. She is a graduate of the Indian Teacher Personnel Program (ITEPP) at Humboldt State University and a recipient of the James Irvine Fellowship. She lives in California with her husband and four children.

This book is dedicated to Richard and Rose Jurado, and to Leonard and Becky Orona, who inspire me, love me, and remind me that "God rewards those who pay the price." I love you. — KOR

Photo by Bradford Rogne

Jonathan Warm Day

(Taos Pueblo) is a well-known artist and writer who grew up on the Taos Pueblo Indian Reservation. He resides there today with his daughters, Carly and Jade, who both attend a nearby university. Jonathan recently published another book of his work entitled *Taos Pueblo Painted Stories*, and he is also putting the finishing touches on a novel.

I wish to thank Children's Book Press and Kristy for allowing me to be a part of Kiki's wonderful journey; a journey that I will now share with my daughters and little Gina Marianna Rubi Bauch who was the model for Kiki. I would also like to thank my friend Giovanna for her photography. — JWD

Photo by Giovanna Paponetti